Miss Hoot

Mole

Frog

Mouse

Owl

Rabbit

For Amber
LM

First published 2017 by Macmillan Children's Books
an imprint of Pan Macmillan
20 New Wharf Road, London N1 9RR
Associated companies throughout the world
www.panmacmillan.com

ISBN 978-1-5098-2842-5 (HB)
ISBN 978-1-5098-2843-2 (PB)

1 3 5 7 9 8 6 4 2

A CIP catalogue record for this book is available
from the British Library.

Printed in China

Lydia Monks

Mouse's Big Day

MACMILLAN CHILDREN'S BOOKS

It was Mouse's first day at school.

Even though she hadn't left home yet,
she'd decided she didn't like it.
Not one bit.

"Come along now. It's time to go," said Mummy.

"I don't want to," said Mouse grumpily.

"You'll like it when you get there," said Mummy.

"I don't want to," muttered Mouse.

"There will be lots of other children to play with," said Mummy.

"I don't want to," said Mouse.

"Just think of all the fun things you'll do and the exciting things you'll learn," said Mummy.

"I DON'T WANT TO!" shouted Mouse.

Mouse walked as slowly as she could and it took them a long time to get to school. When they finally arrived Miss Hoot, the teacher, was waiting.

"Hello Mouse! Welcome to Twit Twoo School. Come in and hang up your coat," she said.

Mouse pretended she hadn't heard.

Everyone else was already inside.

"Come and sit with us Mouse," said Miss Hoot kindly.

"I don't want to," whispered
Mouse from behind her coat.

Miss Hoot stood in front of the class.

"Today I want you to go out and find something. Something special. Maybe something only you can find."

Mouse didn't want to but was worried that she'd sound silly if she said it out loud again.

As soon as they were outside, the other children ran around rummaging under rocks, looking under leaves, digging in the dirt and peering in the pond.

Mouse felt too shy to join in, even though it did look fun.

Owl found some feathers and imagined
what kind of bird they had come from.

Rabbit found a little carrot.
It had been bigger once!

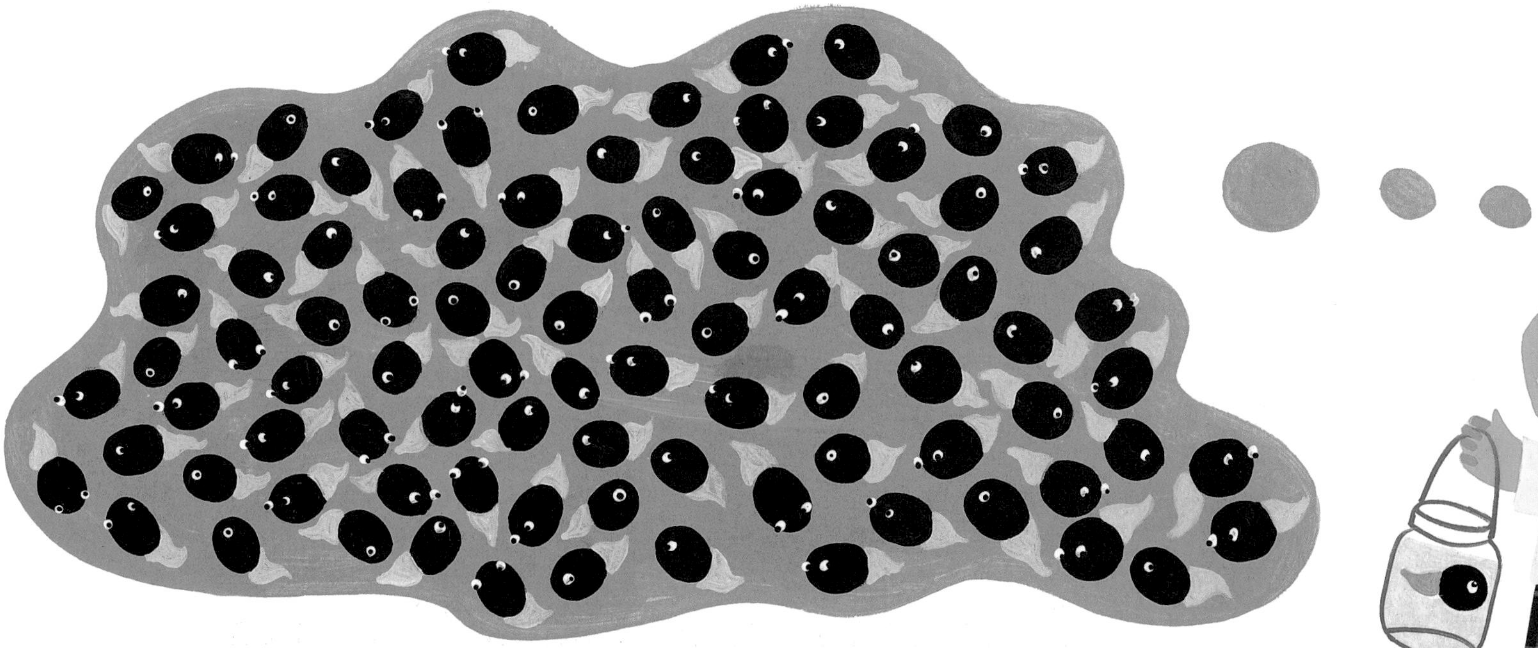

Frog found one of his brothers.
Or sisters. He couldn't quite tell.

Mole found gold and wondered
who had buried it.

And Mouse . . . ?

Where was Mouse? She had disappeared!
They couldn't see her anywhere.
They all had a look for her . . .

... but Miss Hoot knew where she was.

She had hidden in a hole,
and had a little cry.

"Are you coming out now?" asked Mole, taking hold of her paw.

"I don't want to," said Mouse in a very
small voice, although really she did.

So Miss Hoot and the children carried all the things they had found, including Mouse, back to the classroom.

Mouse quite enjoyed the ride!

When they got back to school, they put everything on the table and had a good look at what they had discovered.

Mouse loved the feathers.
She found that frog
was ticklish.

And she'd never tasted carrot before.
She found that it was crunchy.

Mouse thought the tadpole looked funny. She found that it had little legs.

And she loved the gold! Mouse found that it really suited her.

Mouse wished she'd found something special to share with her new friends too.

"Tidy up now, children. It's time to go home," said Miss Hoot.
"I don't want to!" giggled Mouse.
"And I don't want to!" laughed Mole.
"And we don't want to!" joined in all the rest.

It was then Mouse realised that she had found something after all.

She'd found that she didn't like school . . .

She LOVED it, and she couldn't wait to find out what tomorrow would bring!

Miss Hoot

Mole

Frog

Mouse

Owl

Rabbit